D1432891

THREE, WALKING

NIKIA CHANEY

BAMBOO
DART
PRESS

LOS ANGELES † NEW YORK † LONDON † MELBOURNE

Three, Walking by Nikia Chaney

ISBN: 978-1-947240-32-2

eISBN: 978-1-947240-33-9

Copyright © 2021 Nikia Chaney. All rights reserved.

First Printing 2021

Cover art by Dennis Callaci

For information:

Bamboo Dart Press

chapbooks@bamboodartpress.com

Curated and operated by Dennis Callaci and Mark Givens

Bamboo Dart Press 013

www.pelekinesis.com

www.bamboodartpress.com

SHRiMPER
www.shrimperrecords.com

This book is dedicated to black and brown girls dreaming of other worlds everywhere and to my daughters, Salsabil and Juwariya, one who will find the way out and the other who has so much left to see. I love you baby girls. Walk and dream, always.

"*Three, Walking* is a courageous work of poetic sci-fi-lit. A unique collection of short stories that stretch the imagination of strange worlds where women matter, where women make brave decisions, where women walk in different directions, their own limbs indicative of their power to control their circumstances, their bodies, and their existence. Nikia Chaney is a champion of explorative work, embracing the uniqueness of her own style, *Three, Walking* is a fantastic treat."

–Ginger Galloway, author of *Hope for Lunar Days* and *Destiny Interrupted.*

"Nikia Chaney's riveting tales read like focused beams of sunlight through a magnifying glass over an anthill...when we're the ants. Ruthless in their investigations into the nature of human interactions both interpersonal and cross-cultural, but also in their compassion, they have the spareness of generations-old creation myths, and the resonance."

–Glen Hirshberg, author of *Infinity Dreams*

"Nikia Chaney's short story trilogy *Three, Walking* is a testament to resilience as we bear witness to Black's blues, Girl birthing life, and an insatiable hunger to be free and loved, even if it means walking to the other side of the world. Chaney captivates readers with soul-wrenching descriptions of dispossession. Puzzle a black woman's body, how it is valued and devalued and how it fiercely reclaims itself in *Three, Walking.*"

–Romaine Washington, author of *Purgatory Has an Address*

CONTENTS

1. A Small Problem 7
2. Out...18
3. Night, Walking...31

A SMALL PROBLEM

Dearest,

We have a problem. It is a small problem. Look dear, I've been leaning over the keep-pen and looking down at these heads going over and over and over again in my head. Maybe it has something to do with a basic flaw in reproduction methods? Or maybe it's a chemical signature or something? Something we've been overlooking... But well, well, let me explain what happened first okay?

I must admit that the reproduction method is very strange. The differences between the two sexes are... complicated. To say the least. I've never been able to justify it. And does it make the experiment difficult? It is such a waste, having to even keep the males. Takes up too much room in the keep-pen. I'm pretty sure the crowding is a factor in why the experiment keeps failing. Although George, all told it is rather fascinating watching them. Those cottony heads, like little brown puffballs, those funny little bent limbs, the smooth skin, the wide eyes. I've found that I love watching them work. Those limbs move fast! And they are so quiet so strong.

Oh, how I wish you were here to share this with me. All those heads, running from place to place on the black dirt, tip, tip, tip, working away on our effigy. It is quite a sight to see!

This new batch is quite good too. They've got the appendage down perfect, and I know the metal scrapers cut the skin of their hands. I'll have to thoroughly wash the model when they've finished, but trust me, it is wonderful, looks just like you.

But dear, no matter what I do, it is the same thing. The problem of the males. Remember that first batch, when I realized the females would not work without punishment and I exterminated all the males? What a complete disaster. Remember when the females revolted and completely ran amok. That was soooo frustrating! It took a whole day to clean up all the blood and body parts. I didn't get a chance to tell you all the details. Even, exterminating the males out of sight of the females made no difference. No work, just cottony heads milling around the wire perimeter of the cage listlessly, no matter how many times I whipped them. Extra food, extra water, even those colored pieces of fiber they liked to lay down on or wrap around themselves wouldn't get them up and going. Temperature changes in the pen didn't work either. Too hot and they lay there like gassed bodies. Just like that skinny first batch we had when we didn't understand that they breathed in oxygen. When I make it cold and they huddle together. Shaking, rocking, watching their breath condense in the air. But no work. No work at all! And that just won't do.

So back to the drawing board. I put the males in the pen with the females again. But look at this now. Females in the pen surrounded by males, laying about doing no work. Males and females paired up, holding each other, more entranced in themselves... Don't get me wrong, I followed your suggestion. I cut off the males' lower limbs when they were young even though I thought that the males would be able to work, too. You were right... are right... as usual that it makes more sense to just segregate the two sexes. It does give me less of a need for high-calorie food. And yes, these incapacitated males are no real bother on their own. Much too weak to cause trouble on their own.

But you know, I did leave the male's upper limbs intact. Please understand I followed your suggestion but I thought I had to adjust for the conditions of the experiment. The males were getting sores, everywhere. So the males are not truly incapacitated. They could drag themselves around. This was a mistake, and I see that now.

I mean, I thought that if I designated a time for mating, didn't punish the females for giving the males the best spots in the pen, and even let the two sexes sleep together (they mass together like mercury, all clumped together in pairs) it would work. Oh, this problem with the females!

And, I'm NOT getting caught up with these creatures. I just want the experiment to work. Take this really dark one here in the photograph. Not the one with the malformed lower limb, the one with that long scar on the forehead, third from the left. She got it when I took her as an infant. I clung so tight to her that I accidentally scraped her face. I was taking samples of the black ones who tend to be slightly smaller than the browns. This was back when I tried, per your suggestion, of course, to segregate the strongest from the weaker ones by color and body type.

The scrape was pretty bad, though. I left it chained on the sampling table for a few hours, sure she would be dead when I returned. But she lived and I put her back in the pen. I didn't think it important to tell you at the time. I was still having that food problem, remember? Goodness am I glad I figured out the proper ratio pretty quick! Those early days when they fought with each other were something!

Well, this scarred one had this funny way of moving, you know. Probably from the injury. It was like she was hunched over a bit, upper limbs all drawn in close to her body. But she was strong, fit, able to scrape and collect and carry and work just like all the others. Even after we increased the difficulty of their tasks. I thought she would die, though, lying in the middle of the pen, too injured to stand anymore, prone, and shivering and listless, like a male.

But no, she endured and grew very strong. She was very smart, too. Got along with the others despite her small size and the scar. Once, I had to stop the water, as well as the food, and raise the temperature, because the females got together and tried to climb up out of the pen. They got into a formation with the biggest browns of the batch holding up the smaller ones. I came back and there they were, a breathing pyramid of over 35 bodies, grunting and sweating, the tallest blacks and reds reaching up towards the pen hold latch.

Oh, I laughed so hard seeing them go tumbling down? What a riot! I told you all about it, remember? And yes, you told me to focus on the reprimand. You told me that I must take things seriously. But they are so INTERESTING to watch.

Anyway, I raised the temperature and stopped the water. Oh, it was wild. They were all laying there, panting with open mouths, when the little scarred black, out of the sky blue, I tell you, shows them how to drink the waste liquid. Apparently, she had gathered some up and let it distill slightly. She not only went around giving each one a sip, she then showed the others exactly what she had done! I could have fallen over into the pen. I mean all told that's pretty bright.

Now dear, please understand. There was just no point in further punishment after that. I know what you said, and yes I did think to score the external two organs on their chests. That area is very sensitive and any pain, even a quick nick, inflicted there would be quite agonizing. I know you would have done no less. I understand the importance of my consistency with them. But to do that would have meant collecting and punishing all the females individually, and well... I just didn't want to spend that time. I want to OBSERVE. You do know this about me.

Well, after this incident this little scarred one became their leader. The other females deferred to her, gave her the best food, the warmest sleeping place. Got so every time I looked in the keep pen I'd scan around and sure enough whatever they were doing she was in the center of it. I must admit I felt sort of... proud? I don't know I mean they are OURS. You know, like here she was, smaller and scarred but damn if she didn't seem bigger than all the others. Fascinating to watch, really, simply FASCINATING. I'm sure you would agree.

This one time, oh I've got to tell you this, George! This one time I found her making this noise from deep in her throat. Can't for the life of me describe it to justice. It was rhythmic, had this pattern, two short beats, then one beat of emphasis. The males sometimes make tuneful sounds when they mate just before we kill them. You know even when they communicate it is quite pleasing to hear, especially when their move about in various states of physical arousal. But this one time, my little scarred black directed her sounds at the grown females. Looking at each female, working and moving her body.

At first, I wasn't too interested. I had the tests to run and one of the brown males had managed to impale himself on the inner pen wire. Oh, how I hate when they do that! Gets the other males in proximity all agitated. Like they know that their usefulness is only to inseminate the female workers. And oh the volume of those sounds they make! Get them agitated and it's like I can't think high-pitched screeches, then a long low-frequency noise, a moaning, for hours on end. I LOATHE the males.

Anyway, though I was talking about the sounds. After I caught the little scarred one making those sounds, I noticed the other females taking up the sounds, and, get this, working to the rhythm of those sounds. I almost punished them. But damned if the work didn't go faster. They got an entire proboscis done on the first shift. I couldn't believe it. I mean, they always worked together, but this was... well, something more. Even the males took the sounds up. No more wailing and moaning. Every one of them making noises with their mouths, moving their bodies at the same time. They even started doing it when they weren't working. I had to punish them for that, wasting energy and all. But since the work went faster, I let them make all the noise they wanted when they worked. It is quite nice to listen to as I run tests. Sometimes I feel I can almost concentrate better. And all that from that little scarred one, walking that crouched over walk, touching and interacting with the other females.

I don't know why I hoped that maybe she would be different

somehow. That this batch, with her as their leader, would take the assignment to the end. She seemed so smart. But sure enough, I look in one day, and those males, those damn males...

She was making her sounds, as usual. Walking about, touching, or making the turned-up mouth face to the others. Nothing out of the ordinary. I was collecting male infants to immobilize as usual, when I noticed that she had stopped making the mouth sound. She was watching me. They rarely look at me directly, which is in itself unusual, but I've never counted it because they have always proven to be most observant when I demonstrate how they are to work or what they are to do. This time, though, black was looking at me directly, standing still. Her dark eyes barely blinked, she held her body still and stiff. She didn't even seem cowed over or afraid. She just looked at me, her face slack and closed.

I was holding the male infant by his foreleg. He dangled from my grasp. It is such a nuisance having to remove the infants from the males. They fight and struggle pretty fiercely, even without lower limbs for support. And they are not like the females. Eager to learn as to avoid punishment. Males are observant and watchful, but when I punish them they are drawn up in little tight balls unable or unwilling to learn. Defiant, useless.

But this time, black was watching me, so I had an idea. I purposely shook the adult male several times and dropped the infant as hard as I could on the ground, killing it. I've seen you do this before even though we have agreed about the need to not waste specimens. But dear, if I could teach the males not to struggle, it was worth one infant. Black had shown she was smart. Perhaps she could find a way to get the males to stop struggling?

But she didn't do anything, just looked down, took up her mouth music, and walked away. I was disappointed, but not too much. I do know how simple these creatures can be.

However, the next time I looked in the pen, black was with the same adult male who struggled with me the day before. He was one of the smaller ones, red, and taken to making the most noise. I thought it was simple mating behavior, copulation. Overdue because black never seemed interested in the males. Not like some of the other males. But she started taking this with her all the time, helping him drag herself about, carrying him, placing little bits of meal in his open palms. She licked his mouth sometimes and he licked back. They even held hands, making the rhythmic mouth sound. I didn't like it. Black was... well... black was too important. I could teach black, use her to help me control the others. Black was MINE and this would not do. I'm sure that you would have agreed.

I decided to take the male from her while she was sleeping. Perhaps an open punishment would have been better. The other males could have seen and learned. But I didn't want to... well... antagonize black any further. It wasn't even a punishment really, I just needed to remove the distraction.

It was strange, dear. Going in the pen in dark to remove the female. Black had curled her body around his and their breathing was aligned. She had a lower limb thrown over his smaller body and both their mouths hung open. I watched them sleeping for a while. And when they moved in sleep, I reached in and pulled him up. And of course, he woke right up and screamed. Damn male! And then I just... I don't know. All these problems...

And I wouldn't have killed her, dear. I knew she would be agitated, but what she did... She stood there covered in her male's blood like she was waiting. She made one sound, a high-pitched squeak, almost like a whistle. And then they were all awake, watching me, standing behind him.

I actually felt afraid. This was nothing like that escape attempt either. They looked like they were going to come after me. Like I was going to be punished. Oh, it was quite frightening! I could barely get the hatch closed...

Dear, the entire batch is gone.

You must understand, dear what happened. I've done the best I can in the situation, under these conditions. I destroyed the whole batch. There is not even a sample left to repopulate. Even the effigy is lost. I... I don't know what came over me. We will have to start again, with fresh specimens. Perhaps you can pick some up on the way here? But dear, could you clean the pen this time. I ate what I could but I've no appetite for these creatures anymore.

OUT

Girl crouched down low in the darkness of the tunnel. She felt the cold of the slanted wall against her bare feet. There had been no spare scraps left to wrap around her feet. She should have taken time to find some kind of scraps. Scraps could be found, here and there, in the tunnels. Shiny things could be broken and used to cut. Soft things could be torn in strips, wrapped around feet, or shoulders to keep warm. Once Girl had found a scrap so long that Old Woman had been able to strip it into enough pieces for all the men's feet. She was fast in the tunnels and her eyes were quick. But now was not the time for scraps. The Family was desperate and too hungry to spend time, looking for anything other than food, which, unlike scraps, could only be found Out.

Girl hung her head low and fought back the waves of nausea that were stronger than the hunger pain. She didn't want to go out, and she rubbed the new, soft curve of her stomach. Her small joy despite the hunger. The others had no such respite. And despite their awareness of Girl's changing body, they all stared at her with cold eyes. They watched her closely and waited. It wasn't right, that she should go, especially now, but there was no other choice. Girl closed her eyes, at the edge of the furthest place she had ever dared venture. The darkness in the tunnel only increased. She wanted to lay next to Last-Man, in the end tunnel, even though she was the only one that would come near him, and sleep, sleep, like Boy and Little Girl, curled up close to Old Woman. But even Old Woman looked at Girl with hard eyes and waited, too. Girl was the only one who could go. Boy and Little Girl, more baby than anything, were both too small. Old Woman was too lame. Old Man had not returned some time ago. And Young Man, now Last-Man, had no leg. There was no one left to go to find food but Girl.

Girl opened her eyes and looked around. She was in a part of the inner wall she had never been before. To her right, the passageway was marked by old blood and smeared stains. She could remember the gaping wound that Last-Man came back with. The red-black blood had seeped through the last soft scrap that Old Woman had tied tight over the ragged flesh that should have continued on to become a leg. He still lived, but the rotten smell that came from him told them all he would die soon. When he appeared, after dragging himself back, Girl had screamed until Old Woman covered her mouth and held her tight. Girl could remember how Old Woman's thin body had shaken. When Old Woman made the bleeding stop, Girl lay down next to Young Man. Old Woman had left the couple then, staring at Girl, refusing to look at Young Man again. He was useless and he would attract Not-Family. He would die and there would be no food, from him. Girl had not met Old Woman's eyes. Girl would go, but she would mourn first.

To the left was more darkness. Girl knew the way to go. Out. All knew the way. But none dared but Men, who were strong enough to find food. Left, left, then right, then straight. What is out? Girl did not know. Boys who went for the first time came back, eyes wide, the muscle in their chest-beating fast. Men brought back food, scraps, wounds, and death. More often than not, they didn't come back. Old Man had been a find for Old Woman. He was wise and strong, to live so long. But too soon after Old Woman had found him, he was gone. Young Man was brave, he went out often, but he never found much. Now Young Man was dying. The thought of it pushed her forward. She listened carefully and began moving slowly now that she was away from the familiar tunnel. She could hear very faint sounds, scufflings, coming from away. This was normal, in the tunnels, but Girl didn't like the sounds now. She clutched the shiny thing she had taken with her. If she saw others, who were not Family, she would have to hurt them, make them bleed. If she killed someone she could bring what she could carry back to Family, it was better than nothing else. And she must kill them because Not-Family would kill or take her. She remembered how Not-Family had come to their end-tunnel and killed and taken food and children. Many times, Girl had seen Not-Family come. Old Woman had picked up as many children as she could carry and ran each time. Old Woman ran fast. As a Baby and a Little Girl, Girl had always been careful to stay close to Old Woman, not only making sure that she could see the woman but making sure she touched a foot, a leg, or hand at all times. Old Woman had found places for them. End-tunnels with a solitary woman or man, sometimes children to make a new Family. The last new Family had been with Old Man. His Family was big then. But when he didn't come back, a Not-Family had come again. Girl had run, like Old Woman, Boy and Little Girl in each arm. When she returned only Old Woman, made lame by the Not-Family, and Last Man were left. She glad then that Last Man had run instead of fighting. She had been glad that he was still alive, and she had gone to him. Thinking about Last Man made Girl slow her pace. He would be dead when she returned. Old Woman would drag his body away down a dark tunnel. As hungry as they all were, Family would not eat him. Girl stood still, wanting to cry. She put her head down and waited for the wave of despair to pass. A small sound, just around the last corner, made her freeze and pause. She listened, closely, feeling the slight breeze in the tunnel, waiting to hear the sound again.

After a short while, she turned left again, her thoughts on food. After only a couple of steps, Girl became conscious of a particular smell. The hairs on her arms stood up. She brushed the long ragged hair out of her face. She was sweating too, her body sensing what she had only suspected. She could hear clear scuffling sounds, although she couldn't place which tunnels they were coming from. Girl moved faster. The sound of scuffling stopped and Girl stopped too, almost not breathing. The tunnel was not round, but square. The ground sloped at right angles to end in a groove no wider than one hand span. Periodically, water would rush through, and the Family would climb the sloping walls and wait for it to pass. It was always welcomed, the rushing water. They could drink and wade through the shallow pool the water left behind. Sometimes no water would come and they all, suffering worse than hunger, would be forced to move on and find wetter tunnels. Girl was still, and she heard something else, something strange. She lay her head alongside the sloping wall and listened to a humming sound. Was water coming through? This would be good, but the humming was different. Steady like a pulse, instead of the slight vibration of running water. But she was hungry, no time to wait for strange sounds, familiar or not. She must find food. When she lifted her head up she turned around to see a Not-Family, a man, watching her.

He was crouched down low. He had moved purposely to alert Girl of his presence. He had been following her for a while, perhaps as soon as she left her own familiar tunnel. For a second Girl thought that it was Last-Man; this new man was young, too. But this man had two legs, bent underneath him, strong and whole. Girl noted how his coloring was different from Last-Man. He was taller too, bigger in girth. He also had soft scraps tied around his waist and feet. He was rich, healthy and strong. Girl decided that she must attack, first is she was to have any chances of killing him.

She cried out as she lunged towards him, the shiny thing held high. She aimed for his lower abdomen, a venerable spot in a man. She tried to remember all that she had seen of direct combat. Small men who fought larger men, killed quickly or else died faster. Her attack took him by surprise and the sharp thing scratched him right above his navel. Girl had no time to see how deep the sharp thing entered, for he grabbed her wrist, then her leg, and knocked her down, towards the slanted wall of the tunnel. He held fast and used his body to keep her still while he wrenched the sharp thing out of her grasp and threw it backward. Girl struggled underneath his strength. She kicked and bit, flailed her arms, and screamed. She managed to bite down on one of his shoulders with her teeth and she clenched her jaw and moved her head, wanting to tear his flesh out.

He was too strong, however. After he pulled the shiny thing free, he grabbed her jaw and pushed her head away. He held her, almost casually, in his grasp and began to look her over. He waited, then eased his grasp slightly. Girl immediately lunged at the man. He responded by tightening his hold on her. Girl continued to struggle under his hands. His hold loosed and Girl's kicking increase. She screamed louder, as well. The man's hands searched her body until they reached her stomach. He felt her breasts and belly. Then he placed his fist, right at her abdomen, and pushed down, gently, slowly, until Girl gasped and went limp, knowing if she continued, her baby would die.

When she was still, the man backed away, releasing her slowly. He retrieved the sharp thing and crouched down as he sat, before, watching her. Girl would have run, but their positions had changed. He was now in the way of the direction she needed to go. She could go back home, but there would be no food, no shiny thing, and no favor shown at her failure. And she was afraid of turning her back to him. She was breathless after all her struggles, and she could see the blood leaking from the scratch in his abdomen. But he was still, serene, waiting. He raised his hands and motioned for her to come here.

Girl responded to his gesture by turning around and fleeing towards home. She felt the rush of joy at the thought of away from this strange Not-Family Man. But he reached her quickly, grabbed her hair and her arm, and pulled her back, away from home. Girl screamed. The man put his hands over her mouth like Old Woman had done, making her move with him, follow him. They moved so fast that Girl grew lost. She was being stolen, and she panicked, kicking and fighting him, even as they moved away from home. But soon she stopped struggling with the strange man, his smell strong in her nose, the panic receding a little, clear thoughts coming in. She tried to be still, save her energy until she saw a way to escape. She bit down on her lips until she tasted blood in her mouth, and she went limp. She allowed herself to be pulled along and set about remembering the turns they were taking. Two right turns, and suddenly, they were Out.

Girl screamed. Brightness swam in front of her. And difference. The difference from the tunnel like water was different from the slanted walls. Everything swam in front of her and she closed her eyes unsure of what she was seeing. The world didn't make sense anymore. Where there had always been tunnel walls, and end-tunnels and small breezes, there was nothing. No tunnel. Air came at her from all different directions. And the light, the light, a thing she had no name for but understood without knowing, held her, tighter than this Not-Family Man. The light moved and danced in front of her like tunnel water. Man had stopped, and he had removed his arms. But Girl was still a captive of the light. She couldn't move or breathe or think, past the light. She looked back towards the darkness trying to orient herself. She could see the opening of the tunnels, like a partly open mouth. There were new walls that stretched away from the tunnel-mouth and rose up, Up, and away, directions Girl could not quite understand. But she tilted her head back and watched the new walls rise and rise and rise. She dropped her head back to the tunnel-mouth. The tunnel was home, was right. She moved toward the tunnel and dropped her head, her eyes down. Away from the walls, spread out wide from the tunnel-mouth was the floor, smooth and straight, an unslanted tunnel floor. But Girl had seen enough. The tunnel-mouth was right there. She moved toward it, unsure of how to walk on a wall that wasn't slanted. But she remembered she was free of Not-Family Man and she sprinted towards safety, towards home.

When she reached the tunnel, she stopped. Not-Family Man had not chased her. He wasn't behind her. She felt the pull of home so strong, she almost cried out. But eyes had seen too much. Despite herself, she wanted to see more. She had been Out. The muscle in her chest was pounding, the muscle in her head twirling. She could not go back without seeing more. That more than hunger made her stop. She remembered that she needed to find food. The Not-Family man had not tried to kill her or follow her. He had not hurt her either. She turned and peeked out of the end of the tunnel mouth.

From this new perspective, she could see Out clearly. As her eyes looked around she realized that Out was just an end-tunnel. A huge, terrifyingly huge end-tunnel, with an unslanted floor and many, many large curved strange walls. But once she understood that she was looking into an end-tunnel she relaxed. Many things she could not understand, like the pieces of wall that shined bright upon the floor, or the curved and straight half-walls, that jutted out from the real walls. She ignored these things, choosing not to see them or try to understand them. Instead, she concentrated on the Not-Family Man. He seemed so tiny compared to the hugeness of Out. She remembered his closeness, his smell, and the dangerous bigness of his size compared to her. He was only small in the world of Out. Girl decided to remember this.

He came towards her swiftly, growing bigger as he moved nearer. Girl did not flinch or try to run away. He saw that she was not afraid and he did not grab her. He stood close to her and motioned again for her to come with him. Girl followed him slowly, out of the tunnel.

She screamed when she saw the food. She could not help it. Mountains of food, heaped upon itself. Enough for her to have her fill and bring armloads back to her family. Not-Family Man pulled her arm and made her crouch down. She grew angry, hungry wanting the food. She had followed Man quietly but now she could not wait anymore. She ran towards the food. Strangely it seemed to shine in the bright light of Out. It was pale against the darkness of the weird unslanted floor. Girl could taste the slight sweetness of food. Although she had not eaten in a while, Girl remembered when Old Man had brought home a particularly large haul. He had been exhausted and he angrily took the majority for himself. But the Family had crowded around and Girl had gotten several handfuls, so sweet and better than the touch stringy food that came from dead Not-Family. She wanted to bury her face in it and eat and eat and eat. But Not-Family Man kept her back. His arms were strong and he held her down, away from the food. Girl struggled against his grasp, his arms hurt, now. But he didn't relax. Instead, he looked directly at Girl and then he touched her nose. Girl revved her head back so hard she heard the sound it made against the floor. Man touched his nose and then he touched hers again. He watched her and waited. Girl's body went limp and she understood. The smell of the food! She smelled food, but it was wrong. She breathed in deeply through her nose and she noticed a strange smell, like water after a body had been in it too long. She turned towards the food. Not-Family Man relaxed his grasp and pulled her away, around the food. He moved slowly and she could see that the sweet loamy food extended in a straight line along the wall. Not-Family Man was careful not to even go near the food, he sidestepped a thin streak that jutted out. Girl followed him, mimicking him, still wanting to eat. Not-Family Man sidestepped again, and Girl followed him again, unsure of what he walked over. The light made things difficult to see. But she froze when she drew near. A Different Not-Family Man, probably a Boy lay sprawled out, his face still in the food loam. He was purple with death. Girl saw more people now, all of them laid out near the food, or by the pale line, with loam around their mouths. She stopped, not wanting to walk further, understanding. It hurt her stomach because her body, her body wanted the food more than anything. But she steeled herself to follow the Man. Now she didn't want to lose him. Now she realized he was teaching her, showing her how to survive. They passed the loam and dead bodies and stood close to the wall. It rose impossibly high. Her mind wanted to make it a tunnel wall, but even craning backward she could see the wall still rose and rose. It hurt to look and think about this. She kept her back as much as she could to Out and watched the Not-Family Man both hands and arms touching the wall. It was the only way to not feel panic. He too was touching the wall with his body but he was facing Out. He moved close to her. He touched her arm and belly and breathed slowly. She knew to rest a bit. They would have to run from the rest, run very quickly. He turned from her so his left side was close to the wall and waited. Then he nodded and ran.

In the harsh light and bigness of Out Man was a speck moving. Girl felt the worry and want of home of Old Woman and even Last Man but she followed Not-Family Man her breath growing shallow and her back beginning to hurt. She pushed her body to match his pace but he was too fast and she was terrified he would keep growing smaller and further away. They ran alongside the wall. It felt good to trail her left hand as she ran, but she wanted to keep wanting to keep looking to the right to look Out. The disorientation of Out ate at the eyes and she could see in her periphery shapes that she didn't understand. She could see movement and hear sounds she didn't understand. The light, the space, the loam, the weight of her body, the dead, the man running ahead too fast pressed at her adding to her fear. Then she felt it, the break, the sharp pain in her back. She panicked her eyes registering movement coming towards her, huge shadow like a wall itself moving towards her and she tripped tumbling away from the wall. In the open space, she couldn't move she lay on her back and could only look up at –

it -

a thing so large it made her whole sense of self enter itself -

an eye, an eye but impossible the size, the pupil and iris bigger than her whole body –

a face bending down, the sound coming out a mouth, an open mouth

a hand that blotted out everything it was going to touch her to –

Not-Family Man was dragging her leg. Girl felt it but lost in her terror she couldn't move, couldn't get up to run. She felt Not-Family pick her up and the jostle of his body next to hers as he ran and ran and ran to a tunnel a new tunnel like a dark smear on the wall. When they reached it Not-Family Man kept running pushing them back far and deep inside, twisting and turning until spent they both collapsed. It was some time before she could feel the tension in her body relaxing, a real tunnel, darkness, closed sloped walls. He breathed beside her. The pain in her back though made her cry out. It would be soon she knew. Not-Family Man watched her and then gently placed a crumb of food in her hand. She could hear the small sounds of water smell that they were close too. It was a good tunnel, dusty and unused. She ate breathing slowly through the contractions with Man resting beside her. Woman ate knowing she had succeeded. They would live and be prosperous, a new tunnel and family, in this world, a little bit longer.

NIGHT, WALKING

Callow stared at the base of the tree. Here, the bark rippled and spread out as it seemed to sink into the ground. There were small insects that walked, so nonchalantly, over the bark in long lines that disappeared into the forest. The insects were an intense shade of blue, brighter than the blue flowers and the blue moss that grew on the trees. Their bodies were segmented, and each one carried a tiny piece of leaf aloft, like a great prize, under the brush and over a twisted rotting log, deep into the cool shade of the forest. Callow was not interested in the insects. She was more interested in how the color of the bark in the tree changed from a black-brown to white when she used her stick to scratch at it. Callow drew her digging stick across the bark again and watched open-eyed as the long stringy, dark pieces of bark fell away. The underneath, in Callow's mind, should have been just as dark as the tree, but it wasn't. Its whiteness was strange and seemed wrong. Callow scratched again, deeper into the tree, wondering what the next underneath would look like.

The fist came quickly from the right and caught Callow on her head, just above her ear. She could not stop herself from falling over, but once she hit the ground, she quickly drew up her legs. Two, three, four blows in quick succession landed on her right arm, shoulder, and lower leg.

"Get up, you worthless thing", Asusion said. "You waste time staring at a tree when you know we will be Walking soon."

Callow looked up at her grandmother, whose head blocked the scant light of the jungle, and spread shade over Callow's entire body. She knew every line of that old face. She knew those blunted eyes, pinched mouth, wiry arms, and muscled legs. Callow's grandmother should have died long ago, she had Walked past High Mountain Pass four times now. But the old woman lived, somehow. Fiercely lived, stronger than others half her age. The blows were familiar, too. Still hard, and able to make spots that would stay sore for a while, on Callow's dark brown skin, after all this time.

Callow waited until the beating was over and stretched out on the ground. Then she waited a full minute and stood up slowly, disrespectfully, staring at Asusion until the two, Callow now one head taller, were facing one another. Callow never cried out or screamed during a beating. Even as a small child she refused to make a sound above one or two grunts. This time was no different. She did not lower her eyes, and duck her head, either. Now, Callow stared back, and waited until her grandmother's eyes flicked away first. Asusion turned and walked toward their camp, back stiff, head high, old legs moving fast. Callow followed quickly, knowing Asusion's wrath was far from over. But Callow's mind was filled with the color of the underneath of the bark of the tree.

Brem's camp, thrown up quickly on the Way, was in disarray, as usual. The clearing Brem had picked for the camp was all wrong. Although the Way was over ten body lengths in places, Brem had stopped them at a narrow clearing. Tents stood crowded next to each other; the jungle still too close on either side. There were old plants strewn about, and the smell of rotten was getting stronger. In other camps at this time/place, Late Last Forest, most of the men would be out scouting as the women prepared dried fruit and vegetables. But the few women left were still out gathering, and the camp was full of men, getting in the way of hungry children. They should be preparing to Walk, but Brem was spending more and more time asleep with grass wine, in the shade of his tent. He had not ordered anything, and everyone knew not to bother his quick anger, although, they all were aware of the length of the shadows, the lowness of the provisions. For some time now the shadows had grown steadily, longer, and longer, until now they were too long for Late Last Forest, and the creeping uncommon dimness of the trees made every sound in the camp hollow, every harsh word louder, and every quiet moment uneasy.

Callow followed Asusion to their tent, which was as small and familiar as their silence with each other. Callow found herself a place in sunlight that streamed in hot through the round opening at the top of their tent and went about mending her travel shoes, loudly. Asusion, not bothering to glance at her granddaughter, closed the opening of their tent and lay down to sleep. Callow did not want to sleep. It felt wrong, somehow, to sleep so close to Walk. But that didn't matter in Brem's camp. No one did things at the right time/place, or in the right way.

Callow smiled, although she was unable to see clearly in the shade of the tent. She put her shoes aside and felt under her pallet and fingered her private pack. Her mind shifted to her favorite thing, remembering the time she visited Hilt's camp, at one time the closest camp ahead of Brem's, as a child. Now, Callow thought, there was a camp that did things the right way. She had been too small, really, to travel that quickly. Asusion's sister was dying and no other woman in Brem's camp would take in a child, named Callow of all things, who never cried out, and had no mother. Callow had been glad she couldn't stay, even if it meant being away from Asusion for a time. She hid this, of course, from her grandmother, who, if she thought that Callow wanted to go that badly, might have left the child alone.

How careful she was, Callow, to follow Asusion's every step, then. She kept up the pace and bit down on the sides of her cheeks to keep herself from making too much noise. Callow had been born during the time/place of First Forest and she had only known the green riot of trees, the sound of monkeyflys and shepbirds, and the deep dimness of the leaves, as First Forest slowly changed to Last Forest. They traveled ahead, almost running and even Asusion broke taboo and glanced back, towards Brem's camp, receding in the distant, almost reverently. The old woman and little girl followed the clearing of the Way, and for Callow although she struggled to match Asusion's pace, everything was new and special because she would be able to see it before expected.

Just about the time her legs began to ache at her grandmother's relentless pace, the forest petered out. The green walls receded and Callow gasped and stopped, barely noticing Asusion's preoccupied slap. To the girl's left were still trees, but they were spindly and small, spaced far apart. Sunlight streamed down on the dim places between those trees, and the ground rose at a slight incline. To her right, the trees were more crowded, but Callow could hear a strange sound, like a loud whispering, and she could see a shimmer of silver light between the trees. Asusion followed the girl's gaze and stopped as well. The old woman abruptly pulled Callow toward the shimmer and Callow almost forgot herself and smiled. It was water, much larger and clearer than the little pools and streams Callow had seen before. The water, the river, stretched out far between the trees, like the clearing of the Way, reflecting the sun, rushing backward towards Brem's camp. As she watched the water, Callow blinked and saw a golden light, like sunlight, but small and only in flashes. A fish, leaping out and over the tiny waves, slipped back into the silver river, almost too quick to be seen. The girl dropped her eyes then, her chest full like a bowl of water, or joy, trying very hard not to knock itself over and spill. Her grandmother was telling her to fill the water jugs, quick, quick.

As they left the river, Callow dared not look back, she would want to see the fish, want to stay, too much to ask. She could hold the image, and peacefulness better in her mind without disappointment, and Asusion's hard hands. She was too young, but not too unknowing to sense the need for an unsullied memory. And later, after Brem's son, Silt had left splintering the camp into two, one group that stayed with Brem and one group that left, when Asusion had been at her cruelest, and Callow had lived in her grandmother's shadow, like a child asleep, the golden leaping flash of light, the smell of the river, the bowl of water, could be pulled out there and held and looked at, all over again.

As the two moved further on the Way, Asusion never slowing or stopping even uphill, Callow also noticed the differences between the birds. The tall dark birds with the yellow beaks were fatter and bolder. There were more of them, too, and they made angry noises and twisted their long tube-like heads at the old woman and girl in such defiance that Callow wondered for their safety, for no one crossed Asusion. And the rabbits with their six furry legs were smaller, faster. The little girl, who in Brem's camp never said a word above a whisper, even dared to imagine herself stopping and standing still, holding out a few sweetleaves, as she had seen other children do, and wait until a rabbit crept up, body turned sideways in a squat lopsided walk, to eat from her hand. The adventure was influencing Asusion, too. They stopped to make a camp of just two and Asusion broke a piece of breadfruit in half and announced that she would explain the world. The child didn't blink, but sat down, nibbling the corners of her bread, and waited, as if she had always known this sort of thing could ever happen.

Callow pulled out of the memory and looked down at the shoe that didn't need mending in her hands and listened to the soft sound of a baby crying, the quicker ratta tat tat of two women, gossiping, and the loud roughness of Asusion's snoring. She opened her bedroll and fingered her secret pack once again, listing the contents in her mind, yet again, and was satisfied that all was in order. Since it was Late Last Forest, Callow knew what she would find and see on the way to Hilt's camp. The river, and hopefully the golden fishes, the dusty red rocks of Rocky Climb, and maybe even the edges of High Mountain Pass. It would be a harder way going, though, for she would be alone, and Brem's camp was behind in the Walk. Hilt's camp would have Walked further and might be much further ahead. Still Callow was confident she could find it, and if she ran into any other camps, she could show them her beadings, Brem's permission, and they would help her along the way. It was dangerous to travel alone, but she felt no fear, only excitement. Callow turned her head upwards toward the closed opening in her tent. Soon, soon, she thought.

She laid out a meal for Asusion. This time dried longleaves and softened mashed roots. Sleep and soft teeth being the only indicators of Asusion's true age. If the old woman lived she would see High Mountain Pass five times. Older than ugly Brem himself, Callow thought, for this one would be his fourth. She could not imagine what it was like, as only now she had finally come back to the time/place of her birth. Mating age. Only later would she see the world again as she did as a child. And she would place herself so small, in that smallness of the world. And like a child, she would alone, but now moving towards more, towards better as she had never dared dream. Callow moved out of the tent. The sun streamed down, so low, and not so hot as it should be. She watched the camp lazily prepare to Walk. It would be some time until they were ready. Silt, Brem's son, she remembered him as a laughing man, always ready to give small children smooth stones to play with, had a camp that must be nothing like this. He had taken most of the young people, the strong and smart, with him. Now the elderly, the lazy, and the stupid were left, and Brem was a shadow of himself, dim and cruel. Callow closed her eyes. Callow listened to the words of Asusion's story clearly, as if Asusion were awake and speaking to them again. Callow let the sounds of the camp receding, remembered the sound of Asusion's voice, unusually soft, explaining the world.

"You see we Walk on the Way, now. We Walk ahead, faster towards the high mountains, towards the low land swamp, a place and smell you know nothing about. We will go ahead and reach Hilt's camp. But even they are Walking, always Walking, so we must hurry, quick, quick. We must be fast so that we are faster than Brem's camp, faster than Hilt's camp. Point to the Way we Walk, to the sun. Good, you are not so stupid. Do you know why we Walk this Way? It is just a direction, like left, like right. But it is the direction of the sun. The world is a round path that follows the sun forever and ever. The path towards the sun comes back always to the same place. We see high mountain and then climb, low lands and stink, beach and sea, and forest, first forest, midforest, late forest, short grass, high grass first, small mountain, again and again, and again. I was born at Beach and Sea. I have seen the saltiness of the sea, three times since then. Always the same places. Always Walking. This is the Way of living. To die is to stop Walking, to sleep and not wake, to watch shadows grow long, to meet Night. That is the way of death. Your mother stopped Walking, my two sons, now my only sister," Asusion sighed deeply. She stared up at the bright sunlit sky. Callow could see the deep lines around her eyes, as if Asusion was no longer herself, just a likeness, drawn out in the clouds or a reminder of Asusion, lines seen from a certain angle, trapped in the bark of a tree.

But Callow was young, a child and she thought the newness of the world would last forever. She was more interested in something else. Callow said, "What is Night, hama? What is Low?"

Asusion laughed, "So you are stupid, after all. Close your eyes. Make yourself sleep. Now never wake up. That is death. Look at the shadows. Make them long, make them big, bigger still, make the dim take over the sunlight. Now, never see sunlight. That is Night. We sleep in shadow. We die in Night." Asusion turned her head away and spoke to herself, making herself look less real. "Even Brem's son can see how the shadows grow long. Who will leave with him? Who else to leave us behind to sleep in long shadows? But they sleep while Walking. Don't they know no one can escape death? Even the Old Ones, who could live in Night. They could make themselves come alive again." Asusion laughed then and looked down at the large round eyes of her grand-daughter, without seeing her. Asusion said, "The Great Old Ones knew things we didn't. Some say they ate birds and rabbits. Some say they didn't bleed. Others say they were not afraid of Night, and they lived lifetimes in the blink of an eye. Who are we to say, what is true and what is legend? The stories of the Great Old Ones are all different; each clan has different versions. But it is as it should be, for The Great Old Ones were different from us. They came here from a different Way, down to High Mountain Pass, in the belly of snakes that spit fire, from far away. They spoke into rocks and did not fear anything. Yes, they were smart and strong, but even they were almost all killed when they met the Others in that penetrating Night. Now the Great

Old Ones, are no more. They found the Others, and no one could beat them. Always something more. Always more pain. My children were not strong enough, my mate, my sister. I am strong, stronger than they, I will die, too. And you, you. Are you strong, little Callow, little killer of mother, little Walking Night and Death?"

"What are the Others?" Callow asked, whispering now at her grandmother's tales, clearly forgetting herself.

"Nothing for you to know," Asusion snapped. "Bad tales for bad children. Lay down and be quiet." Callow looked away and pretended to sleep, squinting her eyes opened just a slit, afraid in a way she could not name. But Asusion did not hit the little girl, nor did the old woman lay down. Instead, she turned her back to the sun and spit twice at her shadow, pointed backward. The old woman turned and packed their tent, shook Callow violently to wake her, and declared that they should keep moving, and quickly. Callow made no fuss and followed Asusion, silently, their pace almost insanely fast. Callow struggled to keep up, too young, then, to see fear in Asusion's eyes, but Callow rightly sensed that now was not a good time to be anything more than a shadow to her grandmother who did not speak a word until they reached Hilt's camp.

Callow shook herself out of the memory when Asusion, leaving the tent, passed her without a sharp word and an order to complete some errand. Callow peeked her head in the flap opening and noticed that Asusion left the meal that Callow laid out for her, untouched. Outside the tent the camp was slowly coming to life, preparing for the Walk. As I have already prepared, and no one can stop me, Callow thought. There were no men left in camp for Callow to mate. Callow had come back to the place she had been born, and she must be mated. She could not become a wife to the only two men left to mate. One was too young without enough status to take a second wife, the other too young without status to take a first. Only Brem, himself, old, cruel, lazy, ugly Brem had enough status, to take on Callow. But he was so old, and Callow was still young, without any status to mate a leader. There was relief in this for Brem's two wives, sloping, desperate women, could only claim happiness in that neither was the third, who had died badly. So badly that Brem's son had left. At first, Callow had been upset, Silt had always been kind to her, and even Asusion softened her ways around the young man. Now as she watched the tents collapse and fold into packs being hefted on old, tired backs, she understood that Silt's leaving gave her a chance to leave, too. And, of course, she had kin in Hilt's camp. And better, they would know where Silt had gone, help her find him.

The girl looking out the flap of the tent, delaying her packing of their things. She saw Asusion talking with Brem. Their gray heads were lowered, intent. Asusion was speaking rapidly, her hand moving quickly. Good, Callow thought. She knew her grandmother was complaining about her, trying to get Callow punished before she left. It also meant that Asusion was finally responding to Callow's recent disrespect, and eventual departure. A beating from Brem would be harsh, but the inevitable would be acknowledged. It had worried her, how Asusion didn't seem to care that Callow would have to leave, and the knowledge of it had sat between them like a piece of shade that Callow could not rest in. Callow, who had lived with her grandmother from the time she had been cut out of her dead mother's womb, knew no patience in Asusion, only cunning. The young girl moved back in the shade of the tent. It was best to let Asusion call for her. That way the blow would seem to have more weight. Hilt's camp. Hilt's camp.

Callow remembered when she and her grandmother had first arrived at Hilt's camp, Callow was so exhausted she could barely breathe, and her small body cried out for rest and sleep. But Callow kept her eyes awake for Hilt's camp was very different. Right away she noticed the orderly tents. They were arranged strangely. Hilt's large tent farther out, as if it were Walking in the front. The lesser tents lined up after it, from big to small, as if the men and women inside were still in line, ready to Walk. And all the people were doing some kind of work. Mending tents and clothes, preparing food, telling stories. Even the children seemed quiet and in line. Callow could hear laughter and singing, louder, stronger, and freer, like Silt's laughter, everywhere. The women were dressed in bright clothes, that later Callow would learn were dyed from the red moss that grew on the bark of certain trees. The men were all busy, young loud and sweaty, or old and patient. And Callow, seeing many babies did not hear one crying.

When they entered the clearing, Asusion dragged the little girl to Hilt's tent and waited to be greeted. Hilt, unlike Brem came out immediately and sat down in the formal way, holding out both of his hands. Asusion, surprising Callow, gracefully took Hilt's hands and nodded her head. She raised her amulet and showed Hilt the beads that confirmed her status and identity. Hilt clasped them in his fist and contemplated the old woman with hard eyes that showed sympathy. "Go to your sister," he said, making a small gesture that reminded Callow of the way Asusion had spit after her strange talk. Asusion rose at once and left for another smaller tent, not looking back at the girl, standing as still as she could on shaking legs. Callow tried to make her tired body still, she was afraid of Hilt, who had not risen from his sitting position. He looked down at the child, taller even though he was sitting, and held his hands out to her. When he saw that she would not move, he came towards her and picked her up. Hilt carried the little girl into his own tent and lay her down on a soft pallet in a shady spot. Callow fell asleep immediately to the sound of his voice, quiet now, welcoming her in the same formal way he had spoken to Asusion to his camp.

Callow woke in the strange tent and lay still for a long time. She could see all around her Hilt's mark of status. The large interior, the beads polished and ready to make messages, the lines, and lines of drying fruit. The bed she lay on was soft, the cloth woven in a crosswise pattern she could spend hours contemplating. It was fuzzy, like what she would imagine a rabbit or monkeyfly to feel like. When she dared to peek outside to look for her grandmother she saw two women rubbing cloth with moss and berries. She moved towards one young woman, full with pregnancy, as quietly as she could. The woman didn't notice her, talking and laughing and weaving thin blue strands of tube-root together. Another woman lined the blue strands up, one next to the other, and knotted each line together at the end. After she had a large blue square she interlocked more strands to make a large piece of cloth. It was too beautiful and intricate for a simple dress or pallet. Callow watched the women carefully, not realizing that she was moving her fingers, slowly, wanting to learn how to make something so beautiful. The pregnant woman turned to Callow, suddenly and smiled.

"Do you wish to learn to weave? What is your name?"

Callow whispered her name quietly to her.

"Hallow? Receding Night?", the young mispronounced. "Come closer, dear Hallow. Sit with me." The woman's hands were soft as she pulled Callow towards her. The young woman took Callow's hands and placed them on the blue roots. "You make a knot like this. And use your fingers, like this." The other woman began singing. Callow listened as carefully to the song as she did to the young women's instructions. The song was interrupted by the wailing that started in the tent close by. Both women, all the women in the camp, picked up the death wail, except for Callow who watched silently, wondering if she could ever dare cry out such a sound. The men of the camp had stopped working and they stood still, heads down, in deference for the dead. The entire camp shook with the sound of the wailing, and somewhere deep, like the pace of a heartbeat, in Callow's mind the sound of death, was familiar. The little girl moved closer to the two women. The pregnant woman pulled the little girl next to her, holding her small body around the swelling of her large belly.

She heard the tent flap open and turned to look into her grandmother's face. Asusion was watching her, and the sharpness of memory shattered. Callow steeled herself to hear her punishment, knowing this last one, would be cruel. But Asusion was quiet, sitting down to suck on the pieces of the mashed fruit. Callow watched, wary of when the old woman would pounce.

"I have been thinking Callow that you are too old to stay here. You should be married, have children. I see you are packed and ready to travel. You think I do not know about the silly secrets you try so hard to hide from me." Yes, Callow thought this last punishment would be very hard indeed. Asusion continued after a pause, "And I have not been so kind to you, these years. No?" She pronounced each word slowly, taking time to savor her meal.

Callow frowned and even though she had opened the flap and sat in full sunlight, she felt cold, her former thoughts stumbling over themselves to flee at Asusion's strange, strange, words.

"I have been talking to Brem. What shall we do with you? What do you think?" Asusion put down her plate and stared at Callow now, obviously waiting for a response.

But Callow would give her none. Not a word. Instead, she thought of the bark of the tree, the sound of the water, the swelling of the body of a woman with child. Callow filled her mind with the leaping fish, golden, catching the light and becoming tiny suns for a second. She heard the voice of the pregnant woman who had befriended her and lay her head in Hilt's arms to fall asleep. She watched as Brem's son, Silt held out smooth stones for her and her alone, right before he left. Callow was sitting, but she felt herself sit down again, in her mind, where there was no one's voice but her own, and all the images of the past shaded and asleep. Her grandmother's words, her grandmother's victory told her what she already knew.

"Brem says he'll take another wife. You are a bit young, and you have no status, so you will stay here with me a little longer." Asusion shifted, perhaps to get a better look at Callow's misery. "I have accepted the dowry and the contract is made. He has permitted for your amulet to be made. The beads of the act are being written."

"No."

"Your husband will not take your insolence as well as me, you know. Think of what happened to his third wife."

"I will leave for Hilt's camp. I will not marry Brem," Callow spoke these words to herself. She barely saw her grandmother sitting there.

"And how shall you do that, little bringer of Death. They will not accept you without an amulet. The beads are being written. Brem will not lose status over this. He will send word for you and Hilt's camp will discover that you ran from Brem, respected, Brem, who has lived so very long now." Asusion pushed her plate away and moved closer, whispering her words. "When you were born I thought to leave you for the coming Night. I buried my sweet daughter and lay you on the ground and turned my back. Such pain you brought my daughter and for nothing, a worthless girl. But I took you up again. Why did I do this?" Asusion leaned in closer. "I took you up and named you Callow, so no one would want to take you in. I took you up because you are my curse. As I am yours. And there is no Walking away from curses. They follow us, like we follow the sun, and run from the Night. They do not stop, even as we stop."

"No." Callow moved and took up her shoes, her pack. She had assumed Asusion would give her nothing when she left, so her pack was full of all she had hoarded, and kept for this time. Asusion must have planned for this moment, so the pack had been left unharmed, making Callow believe she was going.

Callow placed the pack on her back, strangely grateful to Asusion's ruse. "No," she whispered. Callow moved towards the opening of the tent. Asusion grabbed the girl, pulling her arm back to hit her. "No," Callow said. "You call me the Bringer of the Night. You call me a curse. Then I will be a curse, but only to me. As you will be a curse to only you. I Walk away from you, hana. Even if it means Walking the wrong way. Even if it means meeting the Night."

"Where will you go," Asusion said. "No camp will take you in. What do mean Walking the wrong way?" Asusion refused to release the girl's arm, her voice no longer cold, but filled with panic. "Are you mad? Where are going? Callow?" Her voice cracked as Callow pulled her arm free, and slipped out of the tent, her body starting to run even before she knew it. "Callow? Where will you go? You are all I have left. Where will you go?"

Callow did not walk; she ran. She ran faster than she thought she knew how. She ran in the direction that no one would follow. She ran towards the Night. Callow closed her mind, an old trick she had learned as a child, and felt the soft loamy ground beneath her feet, the whooshing sound of the wind of trees as they floated past her, the sunlight stretched out behind her pushing her forward, giving her permission. Callow had tried to escape, but she had not made it far enough not to hear her grandmother's words and the collective intake of breath the entire camp had taken. She tried, too, but she could not escape the knowledge that what her grandmother had said was true. No camp would take her in. Asusion would make Brem send messengers to Hilt's camp looking for her. They would hear the story and Hilt, if Callow tried to go there, would send her back. That also left out other camps. They too would drink down the story of the girl who ran away, eagerly, telling it and retelling it, until Callow was no longer herself, but a bad woman they must protect the camp from. Of course, they would say, what can we expect from someone named Callow, Walking Night.

Callow stopped, breathe coming in fast, she could not run any longer. And the place she was in was familiar. She looked around closer and realized that she had run so far that she had run back to the place Brem's camp had used before the present one. She could see the remains of impressions the tents had left, as well as the remains of trash, old plants, and food. She stood still, letting the full impact of what she had done hit her slowly. She had run away, yes. But more. She had Walked, backward away from the sun! Brem's camp had seen her do this, too. Callow could never go back, never find a camp. She would be thought of as insane. All camps would shun her.

Callow fell to her knees and lowered her head. She opened her mouth and for the first time since babyhood, she screamed out loud, hearing her voice reverberate through the forest. Then she lay down in the sunlight and slept.

Callow grabbed the hand that was in front of her. It was soft and warm. But her hand was slick with water. She slipped and fell. She was the silver fish, flashing into the water. But the water was held, not flowing like a river, contained like in a jug. A closed jug. She lifted it to her mouth and stared ahead. The Way lay in front of her but it was not straight, it was a circle, the rim of a bowl. She ran her fingers along the rim, and the blue cloth was in the bowl, and she felt the fuzziness. Then her finger came around and she bumped the same woven line. And her finger moved faster, and faster. The pregnant woman held her and Hilt gave her a stone, smooth and round and shiny. "Turn it around," Silt said, and she moved her hand and Asusion slapped her, "Death, Night, Death, Night," Callow dropped her hand and moved away, crawling up, twitching chirping, eating, walking. Silt's hand opened, the bowl stopped spinning and Callow moved her finger back to the first bump in the rim of the bowl. Silt said, "I'm going to explain the world. You are not too stupid to see?" And she did see how the world worked, a turning circle, a rim of a bowl, and the darkness, the face of the Other, walking toward her.

Callow woke, wondering where she was. She sat up, her mind shutting tight the door on the dream, searching for a different reason for the strangeness of feeling. She realized that she didn't hear any people around, and the memory of what had happened hit her so hard she winced out loud. Callow looked around the clearing and tried to figure out what to do. There were no answers in the sounds of the forest. The long shadows, the steady trees. She sat for a long time, blank, wondering if she were dead. Finally, pieces of her dream tapped on the door of her mind and she stood up abruptly, refusing the belief she had gone insane. Her pack prepared so carefully lay close on the ground and she reached down and opened it, removing some dried fruit. She chewed on the sweet tangy taste until she felt the same willpower that had kept her from letting Asusion ever make her cry out, no matter how hard she was hit, arise inside of her.

Callow stretched and gather her pack. She was alive, but she did not look towards the Way. She turned her back to the sun and started to Walk, pretending to herself that she was not afraid and it was as easy as it seemed. What are the Others hana? What is night? After a short while Callow, to hear something other than the quiet and the calls of the animals, begin to sing. She surprised herself and remembered all of the songs she had heard in Hilt's camp. Her voice rose and fell, and the loudness of the sound, the quiet of the forest, pleased her. She changed the tune and sung the song a different way. Then she did it again, smiling this time and laughing out loud because she could spin on the rim, fill her bowl, walk towards the Night. She would see the edges, the other side of the world. She would see something better than the underneath of the underneath of the bark of a tree.

ACKNOWLEDGMENTS

Thank you so much Mark and Dennis for giving these strange stories a home. Thank you Glen Hirshberg, for going with me where I needed to go.

Thank you Ginger Galloway, Kim Martin, Rich Soos, Allyson Jeffredo and Romaine Washington for listening. Thank you all that touched my life in some way and pushed me to never be afraid.

ABOUT THE AUTHOR

Nikia Chaney is a textual artist and writer. She is the author of a forthcoming memoir *Ladybug* (Inlandia Institute, 2022) and *us mouth* (University of Hell Press, 2018), a full length of poetry. She has served as Inlandia Literary Laureate (2016-2018). She teaches and lives in California with her children.

112 N. Harvard Ave. #65

Claremont, CA 91711

chapbooks@bamboodartpress.com

www.bamboodartpress.com